You're All Kinds of Wonderful

Nancy Tillman

FEIWEL AND FRIENDS

NEW YORK

We're not all the same. Thank goodness we're not.
Life would be boring, and I mean—a lot.

And so, when we're born, we're supplied at the start
with our own bells and whistles to set us apart.

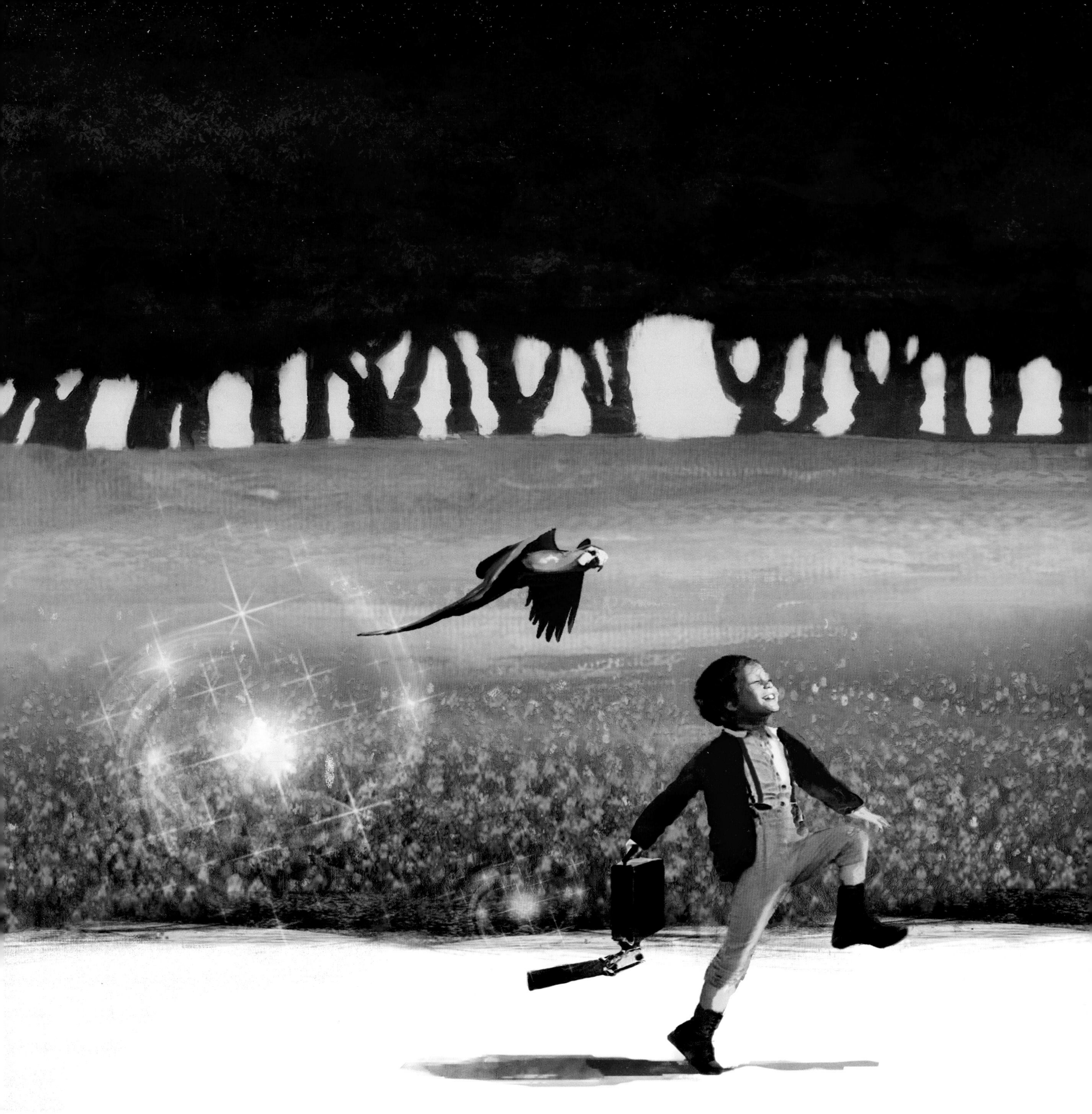

Think of your bells as the things you do best.
Things tucked away in your own treasure chest.

When you ring a bell, your heart whistles to it.
It's guaranteed every time that you do it.

A splendid arrangement! But here is the thing . . .

It takes some *practice* to make those bells ring.

There's lots of advice on the library shelf, like,
"You're an original, just be yourself."

Really, that isn't so easy to do!
You have to *learn* what it means to be you.

You'll try some things on
that simply don't fit.

Don't be discouraged.
That's all part of it.

And sometimes a someone will give you the feeling
that his bells and whistles are much more appealing.

Look this way! Talk this way! Be just like me!

That's monkey business. Don't eat from that tree.

Sooner or later, if you keep trying,
you'll try on something that's so satisfying
your heart will start whistling
and POW! BADA BING!

Ring a ding!

Ring a ding!

Ring a ding ding!

And who knows the bells that are planted in you?
Maybe nineteen or a hundred and two.

Before you were born you were fitted and packed
with all kinds of wonderful—that is a fact.

Put your hands on your hips
and make them both swing.
What did I tell you?
You made a bell ring!

Keep putting one foot in front of the other and there is no telling the bells you'll uncover.

And can you guess what they add up to?

The amazing astonishing story of you.

One morning you'll wake up to find you are grown
and the bells that you've rung and the whistles you've blown
will say to the world that the story you told
was clever and brave and daring and bold—

—and I'll be prouder than words can tell
of every chapter and every bell.

Every time a little bell rings, remember you're filled with marvelous things.

To every child, everywhere.

—N.T.

A FEIWEL AND FRIENDS BOOK
An imprint of Macmillan Publishing Group, LLC

Our books may be purchased in bulk for promotional, educational, or business use.
Please contact your local bookseller or the Macmillan Corporate and Premium Sales Department
at (800) 221-7945 ext. 5442 or by e-mail at MacmillanSpecialMarkets@macmillan.com.

Library of Congress Cataloging-in-Publication Data Available

ISBN: 978-1-250-11376-4

The artwork was created digitally using a variety of software painting programs on a Wacom tablet. Layers of illustrative elements are first individually created,
then merged to form a composite. At this point, texture and mixed media (primarily chalk, watercolor, and pencil) are applied to complete each illustration.

Feiwel and Friends logo designed by Filomena Tuosto

First Edition: 2017

1 3 5 7 9 10 8 6 4 2

mackids.com

You are loved.